Halloween
Hide-and-Seek

Pamela Jane

illustrated by
Julie Durrell

Halloween
Hide-and-Seek

A Yearling First Choice Chapter Book

To my childhood friend, Peggy Brown, who believed all my stories.
—P. J.

To my good friend and companion, Luis.
—J.D.

Published by
Bantam Doubleday Dell Publishing Group, Inc.
1540 Broadway
New York, New York 10036

Library of Congress Cataloging-in-Publication Data
Jane, Pamela
    Halloween hide-and-seek / by Pamela Jane : illustrated by Julie Durrell.
    p. cm.
    "A Yearling first choice chapter book."
    Summary: While playing hide-and-seek at a spooky Halloween party, Jonathan discovers that he has more courage than he thought when he is confronted by a ghost.
    ISBN 0-385-32241-0 (hardcover : alk. paper)
    ISBN 0-440-41219-6 (pbk. : alk. paper)
    [1. Halloween—Fiction. 2. Parties—Fiction. 3. Courage—Fiction.]
I. Durrell, Julie, ill. II. Title.
PZ7.J213Sc 1997   96-11065   CIP   AC
[FIC]—DC20

The text of this book is set in 17-point Baskerville.
Book design by Trish Parcell Watts
Manufactured in the United States of America
October 1997
10 9 8 7 6 5 4 3

Contents

1.
The Same
Old Costume

Jonathan was excited.

It was Halloween,

and his friend Leo was having a party.

Jonathan put on his pirate costume.

It was the same costume he had worn

last year.

Jonathan looked in the mirror.

He frowned.

His pants were too tight.

His sword was too short.

He didn't look scary.

He looked dumb.

Maybe no one would know

who he was.

But at the party,

Jonathan met an angel who said,

"Move over, Jonathan!

You're bumping my wings."

Jonathan thought angels

were supposed to be kind and good.

This one sounded bossy

just like Ashley.

"How do you know I'm Jonathan?"

he asked.

The angel stuck out her tongue.

"Because you're wearing

the same old costume

you wore last year," she said.

A silver robot stood nearby.

"Who are you?" Jonathan asked.

The robot giggled loudly
just like Rosie.

A vampire with long fangs
ran around trying to scare everyone
just like Leo.
A very shy werewolf
stood in the corner
and said nothing.

2.
Guess Who, Guess What?

Leo's mother passed out treats:

jelly beans, candy corn,

and caramel apples.

All the kids took off their masks.

Jonathan had guessed right.

The angel was Ashley.

The robot was Rosie.

The vampire was Leo.

The shy werewolf was

Rosie's little brother, Henry.

Jonathan hadn't guessed that.

Next everyone played
Pin the Hat on the Witch.
When Jonathan put on his blindfold,
someone shoved him from behind.
He felt something sharp
stick him in the back.

It felt like the point
of an angel's wing.
Rosie won the game.
She got to keep the witch poster.

Then they played Guess What?
Leo turned out the lights
and passed something
around in the dark.
It felt cold and slimy.
"Guess what it is," said Leo.
"Guts!" said Jonathan.
Ashley screamed, but she
pretended it was a cough.

Leo turned the lights on.
"I fooled you! I fooled you!"
he yelled, racing around.
The guts turned out to be
cold spaghetti left over
from Leo's dinner.

3.

Halloween
Hide-and-Seek

"Listen, everyone!" Leo shouted.

"We're going to play a scary game.

It's called Halloween Hide-and-Seek."

Jonathan shivered under his

pirate costume.

Leo's house was big and old.

It had a spooky tower

with a staircase that creaked.

It also had a basement

that smelled damp like a cave,

and Leo said a ghost lived down there.

"People go down . . .

but they never come up," he said.

"The ghost gets them!"

Jonathan shuddered.

The house was filled with dark places.

Scary places.

Places where you would not want

to hide on Halloween.

"How do we play?" asked Rosie.

"One person hides," said Leo.

"Then everyone counts to fifty, backwards."

"What do we do after that?" asked Jonathan.

"We look for the person," said Leo.

"The one who hides in the scariest place wins a prize."

Henry's eyes grew wide.

Rosie giggled nervously.

"What's the prize?" asked Ashley.

Leo held up a box wrapped in
Halloween paper.

"It's a surprise," he said.

"A mystery box."

The mystery box looked interesting.
Ashley grabbed it.

"Let me see what's inside," she said.

"No," said Leo. "You aren't
the winner."

"I will be," she said. "Just wait."

Jonathan frowned.

Ashley was bossy.

She always got her way.

Well, almost always.

Maybe this time she wouldn't.

Jonathan had thought

of a hiding place.

The spookiest, scariest place of all.

4.
Ready or Not!

Henry hid first.

Jonathan looked behind
the kitchen door.

Henry wasn't there.

Maybe Henry is only pretending
to be shy, thought Jonathan.

Maybe he'll hide in my scary place
and win the prize.

But Leo found Henry under
the dining room table.
No one thought that was scary.
Not even Henry.

It was Rosie's turn.

She was easy to find.

Jonathan heard her giggling

behind a closet door.

"The closet isn't scary," said Ashley.

"Yes, it is," said Rosie.

"It was dark in there,

and something furry tickled my nose."

"A monster!" cried Leo.

But the monster was only

Leo's mother's fake fur coat.

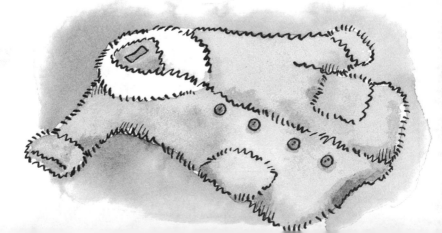

Ashley hid next.

Everyone started to count.

I should have gone next,

thought Jonathan.

Now Ashley will find my scary place.

She'll win the prize.

"Four . . . three . . . two . . . one!

Ready or not, here we come!"

Everyone looked for Ashley.

They looked upstairs and down.

But they couldn't find her anywhere.

Then Jonathan heard

someone screaming.

"HELP! Get me out of here!"

Jonathan followed the voice.

It led to a small, dark space

under the hall stairs.

There was Ashley—or half of Ashley.

Her head was inside,

but her feet were sticking out.

Everyone pulled and tugged

until Ashley was free.

Ashley was mad.

Her wings were bent, and

her halo was crooked.

Rosie giggled.

"You look funny," said Jonathan.

Ashley made a face at him.

"Not as funny as you look
in that old pirate costume," she said.

Jonathan didn't like his costume.

But he *really* didn't like Ashley.

Leo went next.

He hid in the tower,

behind an old chest.

Jonathan was happy.

The tower was scary,

but it was not the scariest place.

5.

A Monster of a Ghost

At last it was Jonathan's turn.

Everyone started to count out loud.

Jonathan opened the basement door.

He started slowly down . . . down . . .

to the darkest part of the basement.

There was only one window,

and it was too high for a quick escape.

"I don't believe in ghosts,

I don't believe in ghosts,"

Jonathan kept saying.

But Jonathan wished he were
wearing a spooky costume.
Then he could scare the ghost
just in case there really was one.

Suddenly Jonathan saw something.
His heart started to pound.
In the corner, in the shadows,
towered a white shape.

The shape swayed
silently back and forth.
All at once Jonathan
did believe in ghosts.
He believed in them a lot.

The shape floated toward Jonathan.
It was huge and scary
like the ghost of a monster—
or a monster of a ghost!
Jonathan backed away.
The ghost kept coming
closer and closer . . .

Jonathan grabbed his pirate sword.

He pointed it at the ghost.

His hand was shaking.

"Stay away!" he yelled.

The ghost floated toward him.

All of a sudden,

Jonathan heard a loud

BANG!

6.
The Winner Is . . .

Just then a light came on.
Jonathan saw four surprised faces
peering down at him from
the top of the stairs.
"Hey!" Leo yelled.
"Jonathan popped my ghost balloon!"
Jonathan looked down.
At his feet was a heap of rubber.
"I stuck it with my sword,"
said Jonathan.

Rosie giggled. "It's lucky you were
wearing your pirate costume."
Ashley glared at Jonathan
and said nothing.

Everyone went to the dining room
for cake with orange icing.
"Who wins the prize?" asked Ashley.
"Let's vote," said Leo.

Jonathan won with four votes.
Ashley had only one—
she had voted for herself.

Leo handed the mystery box
to Jonathan.

"Congratulations, Jonathan," he said.

"You hid in the scariest place."

"That's not fair!" said Ashley.

She stamped her foot so hard

that her halo fell off.

"I hid under the stairs.

It was creepy there."

"Jonathan hid in the basement,"
said Rosie.

"He faced the ghost alone."

"And killed it with his pirate sword!"
Henry burst out.

Everyone was surprised.

Henry had talked!

Jonathan opened the mystery box.

Inside was a bag of chocolate coins wrapped in gold paper.

There was also a shiny gold badge.

The badge said AWARD FOR BRAVERY.

Jonathan smiled.
The chocolate coins
were for everyone.
But the shiny gold badge
was just for him.

Proudly, Jonathan pinned his
new badge on his old costume
and sat down to have some cake.